Margaret acknowledged all over the world to be one of the outstanding children's writers of today, and has over 150 titles published. Twice winner of the Carnegie Medal, several of her titles have become modern classics, including *The Changeover*, *The Haunting* and *The Man Whose Mother was a Pirate* (with Margaret Chamberlain). Margaret has two daughters and lives in Lyttelton, New Zealand.

Patricia MacCarthy studied Graphic Design at Brighton Polytechnic. She specialises in children's picture books, greetings cards, gift-wrap and posters. Patricia lives with her illustrator husband, their two small sons and two black-and-white cats, near Brighton.

Margaret Mahy and Patricia MacCarthy have previous collaborated on *The Seventeen Kings and Forty-Two Elephants*, *The Horrendous Hullabaloo*, *Boom, Baby, Boom, Boom!* and *The Five Sisters*.

To Oscar and Harry – my best boys! – *MM*
To Laurie and James – *PM*

Text copyright © Margaret Mahy 2000
Illustrations copyright © Patricia MacCarthy 2000

The right of Margaret Mahy to be identified as the Author of this work
and of Patricia MacCarthy to be identified as the Illustrator of this work
has been asserted by them in accordance with the Copyright, Designs
and Patents Act, 1988.

First published in Great Britain in 2000 by
Frances Lincoln Limited, 4 Torriano Mews,
Torriano Avenue, London NW5 2RZ

First paperback edition 2001

British Library Cataloguing in Publication Data available on request.

ISBN 0-7112-1561-8 hb
ISBN 0-7112-1617-7 pb

Manufactured in China by Imago Publishing Ltd

A Vanessa Hamilton Book
Designed by Mark Foster

9 8 7 6 5 4 3 2 1

MARGARET MAHY

Illustrated by Patricia MacCarthy

Down the Dragon's Tongue

FRANCES LINCOLN

Mr Prospero was a businessman with a big office and a computer. He was always neatly dressed in a white shirt, silver-rimmed glasses and a beautiful, bright tie. Above his desk a sign said,

You can do it!
You can do it!

and Mr Prospero always did manage to do it, whatever *it* happened to be, and to do it neatly too.

But things never seemed to be nearly as neat when Mr Prospero went home.

"Daddy!" shouted his twins, Harry and Miranda, when he came home one evening. "Take us to the playground.

We want to go down the great big, slippery slide. Take us now! Please!"

"But I'm wearing a
white shirt, polished shoes,
and a hand-painted silk tie
that looks like fruit salad,"
protested Mr Prospero.
"The playground is full
of puddles and sand."

"No, no, no! Now! Now!
Now!" begged the twins,
dancing around their father.

"Woof!" barked Lollop
the family dog, dancing too.

"Yes, dear, please take them!" sang out his wife. Mrs Prospero worked at home as a songwriter, and she was used to lots of noise and to things not being in their proper places. But now she was halfway through writing a song, and she longed for peace and quiet so that she could hear exactly how it sounded.

"We *must* go down that great big, slippery slide," said Harry. "We want to go

swizz!

We must go

swoosh!"

"We want to go *whizz!*

We must go *whoosh!*"

sang Miranda.
"Daddy, you won't get dirty just *watching* us *whoosh*. We'll take good care of you."

"Oh, all right then," said Mr Prospero. "Let's go." So down the road they went to the great big, slippery slide.

It was a lovely evening. The playground was like a bowl full
of deep, golden light. The swings, the seesaw and the roundabout
glowed like treasures. But the great big, slippery slide running down
the hillside was the loveliest treasure of all. It shone like the bright,
long tongue of a friendly dragon.

"Once down the slide, and then we'll go home," said Mr Prospero, stepping carefully over a puddle.

"But Daddy, now that you're here, *you* have to go down the slide too," cried Harry.

"Yes, Daddy! We're too scared to go down the slide by ourselves," said Miranda. "We need a father sliding with us. And a dog!"

"Dogs don't go on slides," said Mr Prospero sternly. "And neither do fathers – at least, not fathers wearing white shirts, polished shoes, and hand-painted silk ties that look like fruit salad."

"Please Daddy, please!" begged Harry. "You won't get dirty. Look, the slide is as clean as a dragon's tongue."

Mr Prospero looked up at the top of the slide. For someone who always managed to do it, whatever *it* was, Mr Prospero was not so sure about doing *this*.

"We need a daddy to hold us tight," said Miranda, hugging her father,

"just in case the dragon yawns while we're *whooshing* down its tongue."

"Well," said Mr Prospero, "perhaps just this once."

So the three of them, followed by Lollop, climbed up, up, up, up – right to the top of the great big, slippery slide. Then they looked down.

"Aren't we *high*!" exclaimed Miranda.
"We're at the very tip-top of the top of everything," cried Harry.
"Aren't we *brave*!"

"We certainly are," agreed Mr Prospero, staring down
the long, silver lick of the dragon's-tongue slide. The whole
summer city spread out beyond like a land in a dream.

He settled himself on the slide with Harry on one
leg and Miranda on the other. Lollop sat behind him,
panting in his ear and tickling him with his whiskers.

"You can do it. You can do it,"
Mr Prospero muttered to himself.

"Go!" shouted the twins. And off they sped, faster and faster, shooting down the dragon's tongue. Mr Prospero's beautiful tie flew out behind him like a banner.

Whooosh! Swiiish!

Wheee!

Wooow!

Going at about a hundred miles an hour, they landed in the sand at the bottom of the slide.

"Are we down already?" asked Mr Prospero with relief, picking himself up and brushing himself off.

"Again! Again!" shouted the twins, leaping up and down.

"Woof!" barked Lollop, leaping and licking.

Up, up, up, up, up to the top of the slide they went once more.

The city glowed like a fairyland in the last rays of sunlight.

Whoooosh! Swiiiish! Wheeee! Woooow!

"But what's this in my mouth?" mumbled Mr Prospero from the middle of the tangle at the bottom of the slide.

"Daddy's eating his tie," cried the twins, roaring with laughter. "He's eating his own fruit salad. Again! Again!"

And up, up, up, up, up to the top of the slide they went once more!

"Let's go down three times as fast this time," cried Harry.

"*Three* times as fast?" croaked Mr Prospero. "I don't mind going a little faster – say, *twice* as fast, but *three* times as fast might be *too* fast!"

"Daddy, why are you looking so worried?" asked Miranda. "Why don't you laugh more?"

"Because of the force of gravity," said Mr Prospero, smiling a little weakly. Then he settled himself and the dog and the twins snugly at the tip-top of the dragon's tongue.

Whoooosh! Swiiiish! Wheeee! Woo

A strange thing happened. This time Mr Prospero really *did* enjoy the great big, slippery slide. He laughed out loud in spite of the force of gravity.

"That was fun!" he said in surprise, picking himself up from under Miranda, Harry and Lollop. "But what's happened to my buttons? Oh, well! It doesn't matter. Again! Again!"

ow!

"I'm tired, Daddy," said Miranda. "And I'm hungry. Time to go home," said Harry.

"No!" cried Mr Prospero firmly.

By now the twins were too tired to climb to the top of the slide, so they watched their father leap up the steps like a goat in a torn business suit.

They watched him slide down the dragon's tongue standing on his *right* leg.

"Again! Again! Up, up, up, up, up!"

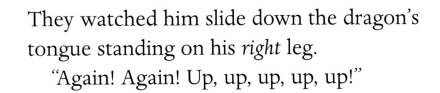

Whoooosh! Swiiiish! Wheeee! WOOOW!

Down he went once more, this time on his *left* leg, graceful as a dancer, his tie streaming behind him like a fruit salad that had learned to fly. The city was nearly dark now. Lighted windows glowed in the twilight. The twins cheered, and Lollop barked in amazement.

"Oh!" cried Mrs Prospero as Mr Prospero staggered into the living room. "What happened to you? Where are your buttons? Why is your tie dangling down behind you? And how did your shoes get in that state?

Harry! Miranda! I thought you were going to take good care of your father."

"He was too quick for us," said Harry.

"I've been sliding down the dragon's tongue," said Mr Prospero dreamily.

MORE PICTURE BOOKS IN PAPERBACK
AVAILABLE FROM FRANCES LINCOLN

SIMPLY DELICIOUS!
Margaret Mahy
Illustrated by Jonathan Allen
Mr Minky has bought a double-dip-chocolate-chip-and-cherry ice cream
with rainbow twinkles and chopped-nut sprinkles. But to get it home he has
to cycle through the jungle, and all the animals want a taste!

Suitable for National Curriculum English – Reading, Key Stage 1
Scottish Guidelines English Language – Reading, Levels A and B
ISBN 0-7112-1441-7 £4.99

I WANT A PET
Lauren Child
I really want a pet: an African lion! or an octopus! or even a boa constrictor!
The trouble is, Mum and Dad aren't keen on any of them. So I must try and find
a pet that no one will mind. What could I have?

Suitable for National Curriculum English – Reading, Key Stage 1
Scottish Guidelines English Language – Reading, Level A
ISBN 0-7112-1339-9 £4.99

JAMELA'S DRESS
Niki Daly
Mama asks Jamela to keep an eye on her new dress material while it hangs out to dry.
But Jamela can't resist wrapping the fabric around her. Before she knows it,
she is dancing down the road, flowing in zigzags, circles and stars!

Suitable for National Curriculum English – Reading, Key Stage 1
Scottish Guidelines English Language – Reading, Level B; Environmental Studies, Level B
ISBN 0-7112-1449-2 £5.99

Frances Lincoln titles are available from all good bookshops.
Prices are correct at time of publication, but may be subject to change.